Andrew Reid, Joseph Crawhall

Border Notes & Mixty-Maxty

Andrew Reid, Joseph Crawhall

Border Notes & Mixty-Maxty

ISBN/EAN: 9783337336035

Printed in Europe, USA, Canada, Australia, Japan

Cover: Foto ©Andreas Hilbeck / pixelio.de

More available books at **www.hansebooks.com**

Border Notes
&
Mixty - Maxty.

by

Joseph Crawhall .

1880 .

To Charles. S. Keene,
this 10th of August. 1880.
Greeting —

These.

Viscera.

Note _ The coloured plates do not specially illustrate the
text, each being a Chapter in itself . _

The Hot-trod.

"The Disturbed state of Society in North-
umberland & the Borders during the
15th & 16th Centuries affected the
whole face of the country which was prepared
for a state of continual warfare — The Border
men were bred up either as Soldiers or Thieves; good,
honest men & true save a little shifting for their
living, God help them: and the women valued their
lords according to their valour or craft, & urged
them on to harry & foray, a Spur being occasionally
served up in a dish at the family meal as a broad
hint that the larder required replenishing. —

The Gentlemens' houses, & even the farm houses
were fortresses; in the smaller peels the upper part,

generally reached by an external stair, was the Farmer's residence, & the lower story was for the protection of the Cattle. A trap-door communicated between the two in order that the owner might reach his cattle to milk & feed them. —

The inmates of the Peel towers were attacked with bows or hagbuts, the discharge of which drove the defenders from the loop-holes & battlements, while the assailants, heaping together quantities of wetted straw & setting it on fire, drove the garrison from story to story by means of the smoke, & sometimes compelled them to surrender. — Englishmen of the one party & Scotsmen of the other party are good men of war, for when they meet there is a hard fight without sparing; there is no "hoo" (i.e. cessation

for parley) between them as long as spears, swords,
axes or daggers will endure. The constant wars
which sent all the able-bodied men across the Border gave opportunities of theft to the "Reivers
& lifters", generally known as Moss-troopers,
inhabiting that strip of land between the two
Kingdoms known as "the debateable land";
men who owned nothing, & whose motto was
"Catch who catch may", hence many who had
a herd of Kine in the morning, had not a cow's
tail at night. -- The inhabitants of the wild
fastnesses of Tynedale & Redesdale had
such a character for ferocity that, in 1564
the Merchant Adventurers of Newcastle en-
acted a bye-law " that no apprentice shall
be taken proceeding from such lewd & wicked

progenitors", the names of a Priest & Curate being included in a list of Border Thieves in 1552. "Saufey money" was a term for black-mail levied by the Reivers on the Borderers for restoration of their cattle & goods. Wardens, holding special commission from the Crown were appointed on either side of the Border, with power to hold Courts for the punishment of crimes, to call out all fencible men between 16 & 60, & to settle all disputes. (For the pursuit of the Moss-troopers the Wardens raised "Hot-trod", a burning turf on the point of a spear which all were obliged to follow on pain of Death."]

The Hot-trod.

Wae's me – God wot –
But the beggarlie Scot
Through the 'bateable land has prickit his way.
An' ravaged wi' fire
Peel, hauldin' an' byre,
Oor nowte, sheep an' galloways a' ta'en awae:
But, by hagbut an' sword – ere he's back oure the Border
We'll be het on his trod an' aye set him in order:

Nae bastles or peels
Are safe frae thae deils
Gin the collies be oot, or the Lairds' awae –
The bit bairnies an' wives
Gang i' dreid o' their lives,

For they scumfish them oot wi' the smoutherin' strae;
Then - spear up the lowe - ca' oor lads thegither,
An' we'll follow them hot-trod owre the heather. -

Weel graith'd - sair on mettle -
Oor harness in fettle —
The Reivers we sicht far ayont "the Wa'." *
Gin we bring them to bay
Nae "saufey" we'll pay -
Weel fangit - syne hangit, we'se see them a'.
Then - on, lads, on - for the trod is hot
As oot owre the heather we prod the Scot.

We'll harass them sairly -
Nae "hoo" gie for parley
Noo the spurs i' the dish 'fore their hungrie wames,

* The Roman Wall.

To your Slogans gie mouth
An' we'll sune lead them South —
Gra merce — gin we cross them, we'll crap their Kames
Then — keep the lowe bleezin' lads — ca' to the fray —
Syne we're up wi' the lifters we'll gar them pay.

Fae to fae — Steel to Steel —
Noo the donnert loons reel,
An', caitiff — cry "hoo" — but it's a' in vain:
See a clatter o' thwacks
Fa's on Sallets an' jacks,
Till we've lifted the lifters as weel's oor ain:
Then — wi' fyece to the crupper they'll ride a gaie mile
To their dance frae the Wuddie at "merrie Carlisle".

A Border Fray in the middle
marches, 1552 — & what became
o' the Meenister?.

———————

Eigh! aa - aa - aaa
Eigh! aa - aa - aaa
Hue an' cry - hoond an' horne — Ca' to the fray —
For the Scots hae been Hautwesell waie i' the mirk
An' left na a galloway, Sheepe hogge or stirk —
Fired a' the haudins an' harried the Kirk —
An' - waur than a' thae, -
Oh! wae till us - wae!
The Meenister's missin' - they've lifted him tae.

———————

Eigh! aa - aa - aaa
Eigh! aa - aa - aaa

Tell't at the Mercat crosse - follow the fray -
Don yer plait - soond the bell - Kinnle the beaken flame.
Up wi' the brennin' strae - wildly the Slogan raim -
Scoor weel the Border - we maun hae the Cattel hame.
        Up lads - awaie -
        It'll be an ill daie
Gin we get nae back beasties an' Meenister tae.

Eigh! aa - aa - aaa
Eigh! aa - aa - aaa
We're het on the scabbit loons - see hoo they flae -
Climmin' yon hill jeest ayont the Craw craigs -
Noo lads - aye reddie - lay spurs till your naigs
An' we'll no fash the Warden to touzle their craigs.
        But - Gude save us a -
        Mischance the loons fa'
Nae Sicht o' the Meenister's 'mang them awa!

Eigh! aa - aa - aaa ____
Eigh! aa ___ aa ___ aaa ____
They're cawtchit rede handit - an noo for the fray -
Belch oot your colyvers guid men an' trewe -
Wow! that's a scatterer - we hae them noo -
An' - as ane expackit - the deevils cry "hoo" -
Tether the owsen, lads - ah! na - they winna stir
Rayther let's tether thae hell Kaimins sinister -
Butte - whaur's oor Apoastle? - Hoots - deil tak
          the Meenister. -

Among the Minstrels & Ballad mongers.

———

In the Eastern neuk o' Fife, there's still living an auld Wife,
  All her faculties unusually cleer —
And, this genuine narration, taken down from recitation
Shows the Minstrel "lay" for twa, three hunnerd yeer.

———

Tak' a King wi' gowden croon — mak' him sittin' in some Toon,
  Feed him early, say eleven — for the dine —
Hint at Donjons, chains an' fetters — set him on to write braid letters,
  An' Keep up a guid supply o' blüid rede wine

———

Gaie Minstrels for to sing and a Harper on the string —
  Mays & Nobles to wait on him at the dine —
Whilst the crowned debauchée a lood lauch lauchith hee
  And, continuous keeps birlin' at the wine.

———

Then, a gallant, belted Knight - always readie for a fight,
Telling every one - ye loar lord - ye lee
But, if any cross his path, he'll fa' in a rage o' wrath
And threaten him with - I sal mak ye dree.

_____

Then, when he's gaun to ride, he's a sharp sword by his syde,
Spurred an' booted - oft a hontynge horne forbye.
And for his leman true thick an' thin he will go through
Though at home he has a wife and family.

_____

At a trustie tree this gemmain will often meet his leman,
If in Town he'll keep on tirlin' at the pin,

_____

Giving way to piteous manes an' grievous, grievous granes
If it's up she speaks an' winnia let him in...

_____

Of faythe an' trothe he'll sing that he'll wed herui' a ring
And implore her to be buskit as a bride —
But, if obdurately met he'll hold out an awful threat
That he'll gar the rede bluid dreep oot frae his syde.

As stern as gnarled oak to his first-born thus he'll croak,
"Awaie, awaie, awaie — thou thriftless loon —
But as lithe as willow-wand when the King is in command
Laigh doon loots ontill his knee, an' cries — a boon.

The young ladies of these daies were mostly weel famed mays
And sae jimp were in the middle, an' sae sma';
As a rule the prefix 'Burd' to their Christian names prefer-
led:
(They indulged much in playing at the Ba'.

Dressed in wab o' silken claith they could rattle oot an aith

And fu' aft they loot their teares doon to fa':
They occasionally wear gowden kaims intil their hair,
While they frequently stood on the Castel wa'.

———————

Such a bonnie, rosie mou, an' rede cheeks like cherries too,
Both their handes an' arms were white white as the milke,
They'd beg new made London bands or ask wha would glove their hands?
And clead them oot in braw goons o' the silk. —

———————

Singing dowie sangs in bowers — often hinting at their dowers,
When their rosie mou's sae aft an' aft were kist
Either by the gallant knight or some lither foot page bright
That — The wonder is they were n't all atwist.

———————

When their hearts set on a knight they ne'er let him oot o' sight,
But make offers to tell doon their gowd monie

/9

Exposing, all the while their bare legs withouten guile
With their Kirtles Kilt a piece abune the Knee.

Wi' fans intil their hands, an' their yellow hair in bands,
And the saut teares aften blindin' o' their ee ;
But, if any thing occurred to annoy the bonnie Burd
She'd express a wish to lay hir doon an' dee.

Then. Call Norway. norroway. and thus weekdays Monn-
                                                 [anday.
Garnish well with haly, hooly, gra'mercie!
Have a cock to do the crawin', an' a day to do the
                                              the
And you'll be well up in Border Minstrellsie.
                                    [dawin'

The Casket

Tune —
"I sow'd the seeds of love."

Plaintively & in moderate time.

Tell me, whence comes Coral red?
Coyly, curious Celia cry'd —
They say 'tis found in Oceans bed —
Strephon — quick as thought reply'd —
'Tis from thy lips fair maid —

Whence those pearls of chastest hue?
Clust'ring round my neck in rows —
I've heard they're found in Ocean too —

Strings - quoth he, outvying those
Thy parted lips disclose

—⁓—

Sparkling diamonds - whence come they?
From Golconda some surmise -
More brilliant gems I now survey
Than Golconda's richest prize
In Celia's lustrous eyes.—

—⁓—

Sour Grapes.

Ruthless Time with his furrowing tread,
(Oh! that we mortals could bid him stay:)
So chills the blood and undecks the head,
That unsaucy young minxes e'en say us nay.

Phillida flouts me _ what care I _
Shepherds still pipe and tabor play _
I'll list to the sound of your minstrelsy
And dance like old Sol upon Easterday.

See Daphne pout, and Celia scorn,
Now that my locks have turned silver grey,
Think ye, ye jades, my hope's quite forlorn _
Alack _ 'twas n't thus in my youth's heyday.

O'er meadows of King cups and Culver Keys
Trip it the live-long Summer's Day,
  I'll comfort my heart with mine own heart's ease
And think upon times that have passed away.

See- my fair Chloris -(She's two score and ten)
Comes- brushing the Dew-drops on her way:
Maturest of maids mate with Staidest of men-
But! ye young Varlets - away - away!

The Seasons.

Tune —
"Ere bright Rosina.

Ye blushing Snowdrops bow your heads —
Your carols, twitt'ring birds withhold
For me no charm Spring's mantle spreads
While fairer Chloris I behold.

Such glamour in her witching eyes
No Summer Sun can e'er unfold —
Her cheeks like Autumn's ripest prize —
In russet clad — bedight with gold.

Her luscious lips and pearly teeth —
Her flowing tresses graceful fold.
Conceals a bosom chaste, beneath,
And snowy neck of peerless mould.

Spring - Summer - Autumn - all combined
Nie not her matchless charms untold -
But - oh! her heart - like Winter's wind
To me, alas! is cold - so cold.

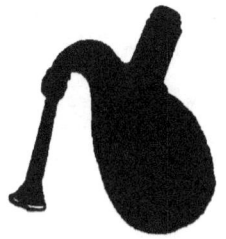

Invitation to Coquet

Tune — "Three guid fellows".

Dear Wat — bein' Vallantine's day
This letter I send frae Rotbarrie,
I've no vera meikle to say —
But — it's 'bout time we had a spring harry.

Chorus.
> For Coquet's fair blue wi' the Sawmon,
> The Ruikeries fair black wi' Craws,
> Grouse, paitrick an' pheasans ca' come on.
> An' fush lang for flees dress'd i' braws.

Whan ye get this — just moont Shankie's naig
An come through to follow y'or fadd.
Then, thegither we'se hae a stravaig.
Sae — fetch y'or short gun an' y'or gad.
Chorus. — For Coquet's &c —

Tell Wullie to moont his naig tae,
He can steal through the Parks an' the heather,
Like eneuch bag a gorcock or grey
To haud three smart fellows thegither.
　　　Chorus.— For Coquet's &c

An' ye'll think o' the wire for the springs,
I' the gloamin we'll see them weel set,
But what need to chirp o' sic things —
Puir pussy ye'll never forget —
　　　Chorus.— For Coquet's &c

Then, ye'll aye mind to fetch tarry tow,
We maun hae luminations at Easter.
I' the dark nichts we'll get up a lowe
To fettle big troots wi' the leister.
　　　Chorus — For Coquet's &c

'Bout loadgins – ye'll baith stop wi' me,
(Routh o' whuskey, sma' still'd 'mang the heather)
An' for colley – nae fear o' huz three
For we're three rael sharp'uns thegither.
　　　　　Chorus – For Coquet's &c –

Sae, freens – mount y'or baggage at ance,
Mind y'or wether eye keep on ilk watcher,
For, to gie thae darned varmin a chance
Diss'nt suit – yours truley – Jim Catcher
Chorus – ⎰ For Coquet's fair blue wi' the Saumon,
　　　　⎱ The Quikeries fair black wi' craws,
　　　　　Grouse, paitrick an' pheasans ca'come on,
　　　　　An' fush lang for flees dress'd i' braws.

":-Step out, Gentlemen. Fifteen years for refreshment."

The Resolve.

[Con o'er my verse — digest what's said in it.]
[If the cap fits — just pop your head in it.]

I know a little maiden, but I'll never tell her name,
Oh — well a day! the life that that mischievous elf doth lead me,
With her arch and roguish smile my very heart is all aflame,
How much longer can I tolerate the cruel fate decreed me?
No more — I have resolved, Stern as Roman, when I meet her,
Irrespective of all consequences I will 'cut her dead',
She may try her winning wiles, but, mark me, I'll coldly greet her,
Aye — disdainfully receive her — for — I'll turn away my head.

Lo! She comes — I grieve to pain her, but my resolution's fixt,
Steel'd securely is this heart against her every winning way,

I'll keep my word right manfully – but, alas! with feelings mixt,
There – I've turned my head – confound it! but she's turned it the
<u>wrong way</u>!
Undone – I'm fairly beaten, and the Minx still holds her sway,
My poor falter'd resolution doth merely serve to prove,
That, how e'er assumed indifference I carefully display
"The falling out of truest friends renewing is of love".

In Memoriam.

To early called to Heaven's mysterious dome,
Hallowed thy name and mem'ry here in love,
One dear heart less, alas! in our sad home,
One angel more with the great God above.

Heart-broke and desolate our loss we mourn:
Oh! bitter words to say — "Thy will be done" —
One transient Summer here, thy brief sojourn —
Consoled — thou'rt placed nigh God's eternal throne.

Coridon's Song

Tune -
"Come live with me."

Come, Maudlin - leave thy sand-red cow,
With garlands wreathed I'll deck thy brow:
Through flowery meadowes let us rove,
Whilst I out poure my tale of love.

All Nature's gaye - the wanton lambs
Crave comfort from their bleating dams:
Then wende with me - caste care away -
'Tis love and Nature's holy-day.

The twittering swallows round us flie,
The groves resounde with melodie:
The little birds now jocunde sing,
And chearful welcome bid to Spring.

The Cuckoo wakes his tunefull note,
Shrill anthems ring from laverock's throate:
What musicke, Lorde's heard in thy Sphere
When mortals such sweete descants heare?

Fair-cruel maid — Scorned love is deathe,
My trembling fate hangs on thy breath:
My plainte regard with favouring eye —
With thee I'd live — with thee I'd die.

The rose in dudgeon vainly seeks
To vie the hue upon thy cheekes:
And jealous lillies blushing glowe
To emulate thy breaste of Snow.

My pride of life – mine heart's desire –
Return this ardent bosom's fire:
If aught on earthe thy hearte can move,
"Come live with me and be my love."

a Rowing Fragment.

Wandering home at Dusk one Summer's eve – the scene Newcastle Streets – my thoughts concurrent with those of that "jolly young Waterman" immortalized in song, a news-boy's startling cry aroused me thus:– "Hanlan's lick't Elliot"; &, not unnaturally, my attention was directed to the 'Great International Sculling match' which had come off that day, resulting in our hero's utter discomfiture. — Though now apathetic to athletics, I was in younger days a rowing man – had a biceps – too – now, alas! limp as Kid – my Sculls reduced to that I'm using with which Delilah Time sad havoc's played – my pairs consist of high-lows, socks and — well – braces. "Happy, happy, happy pair – none

but the ̤ pshaw! you all know that – it's
thirty years since I got what I deserved, as the
fours & eights in my boot-maker's bill bear
witness – my feathering days are past – my outer
form resembles Plato's man : "Hanlan's lick't
Elliot!"– An association of ideas carries me
back to the days of the Clashers, the regenerators
of rowing in the North, if not in the world.
I had been trained by them for the annual Regattas
then in vogue, in which, as an amateur I took
part – What visions of half-cooked chops, stale
bread & sour beer present themselves to my
imagination – what sweet remembrances of
early hours, leaving the proverbial lark &
worm nowhere. – The crew, then paramount,
consisted of five brothers – Harry, Willie, Bob,

Jack, & Dick — supplemented occasionally by their eccentric Uncle Neddy. —

"Hanlan's lick't Ellut?" — A suspicious looking individual dogged my steps — now behind — now on this side — now on that, scanning me curiously. I looked askance, determinedly — following his every movement: at length he broke silence — "Hey! Mister — is n't yor nyem. — — — — — — — — ?" — I was startled & replied in the affirmative, adding "Who are you?" Eyeing me fully, quoth he — "Wey man. divoent ye knaw? aw's Dick!" — "Dick" quoth I — "aye, Dick — Dickey Clasper". — "Bless me! bless me! Dick, my boy (creepy & shaking hands — he was very unwashed) — how are you, Dick?" — "Wey, middlin" — hoo's y'orsel', an' hoo air ye lestin"? man — aw hev'nt seen nyen o' yor crew for sea a time."

Compliments were exhausted - old times discussed, & Knowing Harry the elder brother had joined the majority I asked for the remainder of "the Five Brothers", for by such name the crew was generally Known. "Where's Willie?" - "Wey, man - divvent ye Knaw? Willie was droonded". "Bless me! poor fellow - and where's Bob?" "Wey, man - Bob was droonded tee." "Unspeakably horrible - Bless me!" With bated breath I ventured to ask after Jack - "Wey, God bliss us, man! divvent ye Knaw Jack went to Lunnun an' was droonded tee." - I was speechless - At length, summoning courage I asked after Uncle Neddy - "Wey man, he's deid tee - he deed of a geusse". - "a what?" - Wey, ye Knaw, Mister, he wad hev a geusse -

an' he raved on that way aboot that geusse
a' the week, that his Mistress, though she thowt
Sivin an' Sixpence a vast a money for a geusse,
still, the ahd man carried on that way aboot
that geusse that She went oot t' the mairket
to buy him a one, an', begox! when She
comp back the ahd beggar'd hanged hissel.
Aye – they're a' gane but me – Mister –
an' aw's Dick – Good neet, Mister –
"Hanlan's lick't Ellut" – We're a' dune,
Mister – Good neet." ――――――

Illfluellza.

Bee code's becub croddik I berry butch fear,
It's beed haggig about me low bore thall a year.
What with coffilg, ald sleezilg, alg ploaig bi'dose
I be lo peace - thell, the caldells used, lobody lows.
But I'be wol colsollayshull - there izzult butchpain,
Ald- ah tchew - ah - ah - tchew - there - I'm sleezilg

again.

L'Invitation

Quaff the Vintage, purple red -
To the Dregs the goblet drain -
Though it may affect thy head
It can never reach thy brain!

Gulliver.

Drake & Columbus long at th' unknown Shore:
Vespucci, at his best, but half-Seas-o'er;
Let none presume compare with peerless Lemuel
Or we, in Shipmani right round phrase will deminall.
Adventurous Gulliver, who did Discover
Those well known lands you might have stumbled over;
Secure in port — his pouch well filled with 'rhino',
But, where this brave heart beats now — Damifino.

JOHN BVNYAN, hys mugge
Lo! hereon behoulde ye date.
Wot he used in Bedford jugge,
ANNO Ɨ x 6 x 6 x 8.

———o———

From oute a darke and dismall jail
In Dispond's Slough retreating,
I steddfastly outpoure this waile
To alle good Christians greeting —
Oh Lorde! when.eer Thy sanction joins
A losel wighte and ronyon
May eche descendant from their loynes
Remember painfull "BVNION".

Lines Suitable for Portraits on Porcelain

Queen Elizabeth ..

Wyth ruffe and farthyngale, yn gemmes bedyghte
Lo! heare Queene Bess presented to your Syghte:
Hir effigie to future aege transmytted,
A verie Virgo (withe ye A omytted.)
Hail! Vestal thron'd - fayre mayde wythouten spotte,
ye daintiest Damsel e'er depycte on potte.

Guy Fawkes ..

Oure powderres alle readie - ye matche fayrlie sett,
Wee nowe onlie wayte tyll ye Parlaiments' mett
Ho! Ho! the rare hoyste. Racke & fagote for Guy
An we sende notte ye Kynge & hys Membyrs Ski hi.

If on mug - "Thenne passe rounde ye mugge - Racke & fagote &

x G x   . Hys Mugge.   x F x

Musical note.— The following quotation from a stand-
ard book published on the other side of the Border may
be thought an appropriate herald to "musical notes":—
"Music is one of the most convincing proofs that the
human ear has been so formed as to make it cap-
able of finding a rational & elevated pleasure from
the action of sound. There might have been organs
of speech & ears to hear without imparting to the
ear the power of knowing & delighting in music.
It must have been intended that this gift should be
used, and — most probably — as one mode of praise
& thanksgiving, as well as for innocent pleasure.
Music is action; it is action to some end: the end is
innocent & delightful. The enjoyment has the advan-
tage of being solitary and social. Music may be
made to produce a sense of high moral feeling, & it

may be made to produce feelings of an opposite
character .. It is consistent that man, as he
is superior to all other animals, should be alike
superior in the making & enjoying of musical sounds.
He is undoubtedly so. The human voice & instru-
ments formed by the hand of man include all
the sweet sounds which can be made by all
other animals. Man, by applying the atmosphere, by delicacy of touch, and by sending
wind through the wonderful work of his own
hands has found the means of softening &
purifying his own heart. No doubt music
was given to mortals for their amusement,
and it is their duty to take it in that light,
and be thankful for it." We must all agree in this.
Music is action, indeed we had almost written actionable —

Yah! shut up ~ gerr...out - - - - -

(Further "musical notes" are deferred for the present.)

Matin Song.--

Tune. "Pack, clouds, away.

Arise! love, rise!
Ope thy sweet eyes
And hear a constant Lover:
How fair thou art
Let this poor heart
To thy chaste breast Discover.

The Sun is up:
Each flow'ret's cup
With Dew is overflowing:
The Sportive Lambs
Play by their dams,
And Kye in meadows lowing.

The tinkling rills
Thro' heath clad hills
Their way to Ocean burrow:
Birds on each Spray
Bid welcome day,
And hail this sweet May morrow.

The Summer Sun
Earth's love has won
Thus early this fair morning,
Why should my fair,
Gay, debonair,
Lie, Somnus' bow'rs adorning

Sweet Sweeting, wake,
That joy partake
All nature else enchanting:
The cooing dove
Now greets his love,
And mine alone is wanting.

Pyramus & Thisbe,
a lamentable & bloudie Tragedie.

———— ✦ ————

[*Thisbe, a beautiful Babylonian maiden, beloved by Pyramus. The two lovers lived in adjoining houses & often secretly conversed with each other through an opening in the wall, as their parents would not sanction their marriage. Once they agreed upon a rendezvous at the tomb of Ninus. Thisbe arrived first, & while she was waiting for Pyramus, she perceived a lioness which had just torn to pieces an ox, & took to flight. While running she lost her garment, which the lioness soiled with blood. In the mean time Pyramus arrived, & finding her garment covered with blood, he imagined that she had been murdered, & made away with himself under a mulberry tree, the fruit of which henceforth was as red as blood. Thisbe, who afterwards found the body of her lover, likewise killed herself.[20]] ———

":- Pistol Sir - yes Sir - here you are Sir - Revolver - most improved construction Sir - 6 chambers - two for your Wife - two for the Destroyer of your happiness - two for yourself Sir - all the rage just now Sir - sell hundreds of 'em for bridal presents."

Chronology differs oft in degree
Bet Greek, Turk, Hindoo or Ashantee,
Mosaic, Mahometan, Starkest Fijii,
Homeric, Chaldean, or Heathen Chinee
    But there's one thing we're all agreed on.
In remotest times when the world was young,
When the very first rib from old Adam's side sprung,
In fact in all ages when Poets have sung,
    Love increases by what it does feed on:
With the sole exception, perhaps, of that Swain
Who loved his young Wife with such horrible main
That, the Chronicles say, he could hardly refrain
    On his honey-moon trip from eating her —
(But e'er twelve months - not of honey-moon kind
Had passed o'er their heads, he had changed his mind,
For Eros, we know is uncommonly blind,
    And - (she mightn't digest) - took to beating her.

Then fervently wished, ere in wedlock bound fast,
He had bolted his spouse at his wedding repast.
But this is all fringe – to our tale – then know
What happened two lovers long ages ago.
Aye –

      Years ago – long years agone
      Dwelt in the City of Babylon,
      A fair brown maid with a beaming eye,
      With two in fact – common destiny,
      And a nose between of that Tapir form
      To this day by God's chosen people worn:
This be the name of this lovely 'cuss',
And the very next door lived one Pyramus.
Now we know what oft haps when a strapping young
                       blade
Lays siege to the heart of an amorous maid
Ignoring the proverb of "two of a trade"
      Their thoughts only ran on unition,

And though they both lived in precocious clime,
Like Cæsar's old wife of a much later time,
  They were both far beyond Suspicion.
Yet love will creep in, and love will peep out,
And soon turn young lovers' hearts quite inside out,
How'er he may languish - how'er She may pout,
  In spite of all parents opposing,
So without further fuss
All was sealed with a buss,
And the lusty, and loving, and loved Pyramus
  Was accepted at once on proposing.
Now, their parents suspecting something was astir,
Made each of the lovers a close prisoner
In his and her chamber, the match to defer
  As they both were too young - under twenty:
But, though love is a compound of vows, sighs & swoons,

Turning old fools to bigger ones – young ones to spoons,
Singing sad serenades to the softest of tunes,
    Callus we devices 't has plenty.
When the old folks went out for a ride or a stroll,
P went hammer and tongs at it, making a hole
Through the wall that excluded his idol of soul
    From his earnest and amorous glances.
Then they billed & cooed snugly from morning till night,
And arranged pleasant interviews – oft by moonlight,
Defying parental authority quite –
    Pleasure stolen, it's value enhances.

Years ago, longer years agone
Than any we've hitherto touched upon
Semiramis builded at Babylon
A tomb for her good man Ninus.

55

It was at this tomb on a Summery night
(These lovers had vowed their joint troths to plight.
And freely indulge in "Love's purple light,"
          With a feeling their parents were - minus,
(The time had been fixed - (just a quarter past nine)
(For mutual enfolding at Ninus's Shrine,
Each to swear - "I'll be yours, if you will be mine":
          She was there - but found Pyramus - absent:
Now - whether he thought himself too superfine
(To keep an appointment, or, whether with wine
He'd been overtaken, one can't now divine,
          If the latter - she'd surely a cab sent.
Suffice it say, (Thisbe waited alone,
And was startled on hearing an agonized moan.
So whence it proceeded forthwith must be shown,
(Then listen : —

Cruising along a young heifer had strayed,
A real, live heifer — (I don't mean the maid —
Though it may be with strictest propriety said,
          Maids by night should n't stroll out alone.)
A lioness also was out on the prowl,
Having breakfasted early she felt herself "howl";
So sprang on the heifer with resonant growl
          And eat her up body and bone.
Scared Thisbe then fled in such terrible fright,
(Wan and pallid her face as the palest moonlight)
That her raven locks, standing already upright
'Gan to turn, and turned on, until perfectly white,
Such things have been known to occur in one night
          But this happen'd the time it takes telling.
The beast then pursued her — away went her shawl,
Away went her pannier, her tunic, and all,

Her padding – her chignon – and God knows what all,
Though she got safely off with her chief corporal,
    Clotho'd not yet decreed what her fate is.
Then straight her pursuer began to address
Attention t'above scheduled items of dress,
Seized, and made every one in the bloodiest mess,
Till the chignon espying – in poignant distress
    A header she took in Euphrates.

. . . .

At length to the trysting place Pyramus came,
Conning over apologies – excuses lame,
And racking his brains to bamboozle his flame
    As Jael of old cozened Sisera:
But finding her garments beclotted with blood
It flashed through his mind that in all likelihood
Some one'd slaughtered the maiden he'd tenderly wooed,

And his longing to join her could not be withstood,
So at once he 'made tracks' for a neighbouring wood,
Searched, and found out a mulberry - (tree understood)
The fruit of which, since, has been colour o' blood,
      And under it let out his viscera.

. . . .

Now, feeling she'd suffered a most grievous wrong,
In agony Thisbe came wailing along,
(For - like to "Jack Robinson" - (popular song),
      Dead at all, d'ye see, she'd ne'er been -
When, spying her lover's cold corpse on the ground
With a sword run right through, sticking out of the wound,
One - two - three - she jumped on with a vigorous bound,
      And thus ended the tragical scene .

In Memoriam

Izaak Walton.

Blest be thy memory, Father of Anglers,
Ne'er shall it perish whilst we can throw line :
Aloof from our ranks keep all scoffers & wranglers,
May no worthless pilgrim e'er sully thy shrine :
Green grow the grass o'er thy last silent resting place,
Peace to thy ashes – we honour thy name :
Long since thou'st reached the good Christian's trysting-place,
Here thou'st a niche in the Temple of Fame.

More Porcelain Portraits
Izaak Walton

Who's honest face d'ye heare see? Oh! good lacke:
'Tis rare olde Izaak's — pannier at his backe:
Readie for Barbel, Chubb, or wilie Troute —
Beware, ye finnie tribes — he'll hooke ye oute:
Not hookes alone, but Hooker's life he writ,
Herbert & Wotton also show'd his wit —
Good Bishop Sanderson & far famb'd Donne
Will shine immortal when this goode man's gone:
Seeke to be like him — eschewe vice and riot,
Take his advice & "Study to be quiet,"
And when to Angling Sporte you chance to goe
May y^e Keene East winde ever cease to blow.
His Compleat Angler must not be forgot —
But who this far famb'd Booke has studied not?

[Great Store of impudence - oft small of wit]
[In every age & clime this cap will fit. -]
Great Son of Momus, hail! jingle thy cap & bell -
Vive le farceur - et, vive la bagatelle -
Yorick in thee still lives - (Yorick of yore
Who's wont's to "set the table on a roar.")
E'en cynics smile - thou melts the misanthrope,
Thou screaming farce: thou live Kaleidoscope.
As in the grove the mock-bird's mimic note
Pleases at first - but, parrot-like by rote,

Grows stale apace, so thine i' the busy town
Soon palls - thou'st no note of thine own:
At thy own ribald jests thou grins & brays,
Winks, tongue protrudes, & gasping, fugles praise.
To thee on foolscap I indite this sonnet,
Go, change thy fool's cap for some other bonnet.

Hark to the mocking birds note -
He mimics all birds in the town -

Like a parrot he chatters by rote -
'Cause he has'nt a note of his own.

A Lay of Rimside

"Man, Jock! the heather crop is grand the year.
But, eh! provisions is uncommon dear."
(Thus Rimside Rab to Heather Jock held forth,
Twa muirland besom makers i' the north.)
"What gars ye undersell, an' spoil the trade?
A besom at a penny ne'er was made,
We baith ha'e to provide for wives an' weans,
An' 'tween us twae we ha'e them i' the teens,
'Deed was't na for the lifts we've noo an' then,
Sec as some chancie geusse or chuckie hen,
Aw canna for the verra warld conceive
How honest families contrive to live:
Sell at a penny! man, it's just a sin,
The stuff coosts mair afore it's gethered in.

Thir's no the guid auld times that we hae seen,
The competition's noo that awfu' keen,
There's no an honest leevin' to be made
In besom, pans, or ony ither trade:
Aw steal my heather – steal my shanks an' bands,
But fairly work them wi' industrious hands,
An' yet nae profit at three-ha'pence earn,
Hoo ye sell at a penny aw've to learn".
"Daft gowk" quo' Jock, "wark's nae pairt o' my trade,
Aw never fash't – aw steal mine ready-made".

Birth-day

Alack! Oh alack, & well-a-day!
How old Time keeps crawling on:
Me seemeth it was but yesterday
That I wished you joy on your last birth-day.
Let me see - you'll be twenty-one.

Another year past; and another birth-day!
It is meet then I should address you.
Dear —— my friend - I've but little to say -
Just three simple words: - "God bless you."

Dinna forget.

There's a very large washing to go to the tub,
Both the cook & the household will be in a fret,
So you have my permission to dine at the club;
For - here you'll get nothing - so - Dinner forget.

Dives, Crœsus & Cᵒ (Limited?)

["Thou fool, this night thy soul shall be required of thee. (Then
whose shall those things be which thou hast provided? _Luke xii. 20]

What though in life so keen and hard of heart —
All pleasures here, save love of dross, he'd stint —
Dives — now dead — his gold & he must part:
The shroud's a garment with no pocket in't.
What now avails this great parade of woe?
Cloaks, hat-bands, hatchments, plumes, & kerchers white,
This hollow pomp of rich, funereal show,
Those hireling mourners — seemingly contrite.

:- "Well! I never knew where they all came from before!"

Who, in his heart, for Dives truly grieves?
The mainest question oft – 'how goes the pelf?'
His scatter'd god adored – in't each believes,
But each, expectant, 's quite absorb'd in self.
   For this he's eager moil'd from very birth:
   He cumbers now six feet of better earth.

Worm - fishing

The flee's been sung in mony a strain,
The mennum oure an' oure again
Has been the Poet's theme:
Gentles, and pastes, and viler roe
Hae had their praises sung enow
In drumlie verse and stream.
But let us sing the worm in June,
Auld Coquet crystal clear,
All leafy Nature's now in tune —
Now doth true skill appear.
Sae moyly an' coyly
Steal on the gleg-e'ed trout,
He sees ye, an' flees ye —
Gif no — ye'll pick him out.

Just as the early, tuneful lark,
Dame Nature's vocal chapel-clerk,
Carols his hymn of praise,
Just as the dews frae flowers distil,
And air recovers frae night's chill,
Thro' Phœbus' slantin' rays:
Wi' weel graith'd gear up stream then hie,
Unerring cast the lure,
The barely covered spankers lie
Unwatchfully secure.
Then lungin' an' plungin'
You feel the finny prize,
Now gantin' an' pantin'
Stretched on his side he dies.

Straight as a sapling fir your wand,
Mid-teens o' feet, an' light to hand,

With hook of ample size,
Inserted just below the head
Of worm, well scoured and purplish red,
Like arrow sourceward flies.
Swift with the current see it wear,
Then trembling, mid-stream stay,
That instant, strike.. my life, he's there,
At leisure creelward play.
Then stay there, an' play there,
Enjoy thy latest cast,
For the worm aye in turn aye
Will conquer a' at last.

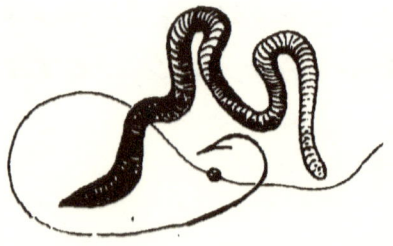

An Angler's Reverie.

air – "Come live with me."

How pleasante on a sweet Spring morne,
When dew'drops linger on the thorne,
When primrose banks, and honied bowers
Are kiss'd by sweetest April showers

Through flow'ry meades to wende our waie,
When sunrise welcomes the sweete daie,
At chrystal brooks our thirste t'assuage
And worship God through Nature's page.

With angle-rod and lightsome hearte,
Our conscience cleare, we gaie departe
To pebbly brooks & purling streams:
No canker't care disturbs our dreames.

Oh! Surely virtuous must be
That crafte where Nature mirrors Thee:
On every side we see Thy power,
From craggy rocke to simple flower.

Whilst under shady Sycamore,
Regardless of each fleeting houre
Some deare friend's converse we enjoy
Our earthlie bliss has no alloy.

From Summer Sun's oppressive heate,
From worldlie cares a short retreate,
Indulging freely in vain dreames
Of Halcyon daies by murm'ring streams.

A Bunch o' Posies &c...

Love me & leave me not + God above increase our love

This littel rynge my hearté dooth brynge + God alone made us too one

Thó fancy sleepe my love is deep + { The deeper the sweeter
                                    { I'll be judgd by St Peter. }

Lett us abide till death divide + No recompence but remembrance

In God alone we two are one + Sumus umbra (on Sundial)

Constancy and heaven are round }
And in this the emblem's found }

(Take time while time is for time will away. —

Never delay the work of to day. + I lyke my choyse.

Ly downe to reste   ⌉   Ladies all I pray make free

And think to have   And tell me how you like my tea.

Thy sleepe thy dethe   + L' Amitié c'est L'amour

Thy bed thy grave. ⌋   sans ailes. —

I coo and pine & neer shall be att reste

(Tyll I come to thee, dearest, sweetest, blest. (best)

Tow faythe full heartes united

To supply the poores neede, Is charitie indeede.

Good morrow, Valentine + { The guift is small
                            But love is all..

Brisk be to the Med you desier } Love
  As hir lov you may requier.   } &
                                  } Happily
                                    +
First love Christ that died for thee } Let us share
Next to him love none but me.   } In joy & care

Knit in one } United hearts } { A faithful Wife
By Christ alone } + Death only parts } + { Preservoeth life

In Christ & thee } { This and the giver }
My comfort be   } + { Are thine for ever. }

This hath alloy, my love is pure + The diamond is within.

I'll win and wear you + Lett lykynge laste.

Virtue passeth riches + { As God decreed }
                          { So we agreed }

Rowan tree an' rede threed, Put the witches to their spied.

A whistling woman and a crowing hen }
Are the biggest plagues that are sent to men }

I goe my waie, thou goest thine,⎫ I will be
Many ways we wende :   ⎬+ yours
Many days and many ways   ⎬ While breath
Ending in one end . .   ⎭ endures.
I've read & I've turned over many dull books,⎫
And changed them as oft as I durst:
But of all the dull books that ever I read
Most certainly this is the worst.
'Tis in your will,⎫ ⎧ Our contracte
To save or kill..⎭ + ⎨ Was heaven's acte.
God our love continue ever, That we in heaven may live together.
Wear me out, Love shall not waste, Love beyond Tyme styll is placed.
As you sit by my fire yourself for to warm,
Take hede that your tung dooth y'r neighbour no harm.
(Focus est centrum amoris _ (The hearth is the heart's focus.)
Nunc mei, mox hujus, Post mortem, nescio cujus.
Nunc mea, mox hujus, Sed postea, nescio cujus.

Ladies stock and tend your hive | Come taste from my teapot
Trifle not at thirty five | Yourself for to warm
Lonesome tabbies should you be | But take heed that yr tongue
Take comfort in a cup o' tea. | Doth yr neighbour no harm.

Why't owt baptysme no sall ma be saved.

Greatness and goodness here at once are seen,

Sweetly inthroned in his/her majestic mien :

How mild, yet awful, piercing, yet serene.

Mulier viro Subjecta esto.+ { My dearest Betty / Is good and pretty. }

Parting is payne, when love dooth remayne.

There is no other, and I am he } My corn is growne
That loves no other, and thou art she } Love reape thy owne

If thee does n't work, thee shan't eat.

Pensez de lui par que je suis ici.

My worldlie joye, alle my truste | God dyd decree
Herte, thought, lyfe and luste } Oure unitie.

My Soul will keep thine company to heaven.

Suilk als ꝥ ai brued, now haꝥ ai dronken. —

In God and thee, my joye shall be. —

God saw thee, most fit for me. —..—

Ande thys alsoe will passe awaie. —

Let Death lead love to rest.+ Too light
                                To requite.

Thy want my woe.+ The want of thee is grief to me.

Parting givest sorest pain }—
Still our friendship will remain }—
Parting giveth us sore paine, —
But oure love will styl remayne }

So put on your night caps, and keep your heads warm,
A little more liquor will do us no harm. —

A jovial Swain   That what I say is right.
May rack his brain
And tax his fancy's might }   This verse contains
To quiz is vain,   every letter in the
  For 'tis most plain }   language except E.

"Here's a health to all those that we love:
Here's a health to all those that love us:
Here's a health to all those that love them
That love those that love them that love us."

Deft limned in truthfull teinctures see
These gaie, aperient flowers
Whereon my little busy bee
I improoved ye shining hours.   Is.Wa.(Watts.)

"If wisdom's ways you wish to keep,
Five things observe with care,
Of whom you speak - to whom you speak
Of what - and when - and where."
    Lof - Godt - van - al - Ao 1647.

Oft wine's praises have been sung,
Come, once more join our refrain:
Tho' t may loose the Dullard's tongue
It can never reach his brain . —

These may be of use to somebody - the friend who
gave them to me paid half a guinea for them :-
To weld cast steel. - "1 ounce Salts of Prunella - 3 oz.
borax. melted together & used to steel as sand to iron."
To harden steel tools :- "4 ounces Salts of Prunella (i.e.
clarified salt petre - 8ᵈ pᵣ ℔.) dissolved in each gallon
of water. Make the tool blood red hot & dip it
in the above solution, after which, reduce the
temperature of the tool to blue: then plunge im-
mediately in the Solution . -

Note for Newcastle Anglers:- "Nun's gate Sepᵣ 9
                                        1830.
" Dear Garrett _ Do you let the threatening rain
Prevent us joining with the fishing train,
                                    (?)
Or V. V. Spite of weather, foul or fair,
By the Tyne Steamer to the Slake* repair (Jarrow)
                                            *
Please answer by the bearer - yes or no -
                                    yours truly
Say - Shall we stay at home - or Shall we go - Thomas Brown."

Inscribed in the first edition of the Countesse of
Pembroke's "Arcadia" by Sir Philippe Sidnei —
London printed for William Ponsonbie A° Dom. 1590.
" Hir being was in hym alone   (on reverse
   And he not being, Shee was none   of fol. 311
   They liv'd one lyfe, one lyfe they dyed."
" King Solomon, young — practised vice in variety —
   (Famed for Wisdom — Wealth — Wickelness — Ladies' Society.
   But in time he grew aged, and could'nt go on —
   Then 'gan hedging and singing he'd done very wrong —
   Oh! so awfully — dreadfully — horribly wrong —
   See first Kings. Chap: eleven — next "Proverbs & Song".
   Note — This was'nt in the Arcadia".
" The eye finds — the hearte choosyth —
   The hande binds — but deathe looseth.
In 1853 I purchased an early Shakespeare quarto.
" Mr William Shakspeare His Historie of King Lear

commencing on Signature B, finishing on Sig: L. 4 -
FINIS. Printed for Nathaniel Butter and are to be
Sold at his Shop in Pauls church yard at the Signe of
the Pide Bull neere S: Austins gate - 1608. It contains
numerous M.S. corrections in a contemporary hand & I
jot them down here :- (I have placed them above the text.)

B. 4. 2ⁿᵈ line from bottom - "Gods gods tis strāge that from their <u>couldst</u> ^{cold}

Reverse Sig D. 9ᵗʰ line from bottom - "I should be <u>false</u> perswaded" ^{halfe}

D°. - 3° from <s>top</s> ^{bottom} - "you are old & reverend should be" ^{you} ^

D. 2. 3ⁿᵈ from top - "be <u>then</u> desired by her that else s. ^{you}

D°. 12ᵗʰ from bottom - "and from her <u>derogate</u> body & ^{degenerate}

two lines lower. "that it may live & be a <u>thwart dissnatur'd &</u> ^{Thwart dissfeatur'd}

D. 4. 14ᵗʰ from bottom - "and thou <u>must</u> make a dullard & ^{maist}

E. 2. 11ᵗʰ from bottom. "to strike at me upon his <u>misconstruction</u> ^{misconstruction}

D°. - reverse - 2° from top - "you <u>reverent braggart</u> - ^{queir old}

E. 3. Edgar's speech - 5ᵗʰ line - "<u>Dost</u> not attend & ^{Doth}

D° - "Blanket my loynes <u>else</u> all my hair with knots ^{tye}

F. 2 . 4th line _ " To Knee <u>to</u> his throne &c _ _ .

G . 9th from bottom _ Thou thinkst tis much that this <u>truculent</u> <s>crulentious</s>

G. 3 . reverse _ 8th & 9th from bottom _ " a horses health &c <u>heeles</u>

G. 4 . rev. 7th from bottom " What will hap more tonight " <u>hap</u>

H. 10th from top " Sir & thirtie of his Knights hot <u>questrits</u> after <u>Coystrille</u> <s>questions</s>

H rev . 15 from top _ " In his anynted flesh rash boarish fangs <u>ovsh</u>

F 2 _ 14th from top " She gave strange <u>aliads</u> & most speaking &c <u>eylids</u>

I . 3 . 12th from top _ " Jew masts at <u>each</u> make not the &c <u>least</u>

2°.   " which thou hast perpendicularly fell " <u>fallne</u>

2. rev . " & <u>do</u> shake the head <u>heare</u> of pleasure's name _ <s>does</s> <u>hearing</u>

K rev. 1st & 2° line top _ " Your wife (so I would say) <del>ft</del> your affectionate

<u>And for you her owne</u> for <u>venter</u>   } servant, Goneril <u>venturing</u>

K 2 8th from bottom _ Sir Know <u>you</u> me . _ L. 5th from bottom ^{rev.}

" Conspicuate gainst this high, illustrious Prince ." _ <u>Conspirator against</u>

L. 4. 19 from bottom " Should a dog, a horse, a rat <u>of</u> life . . <u>have</u>

I sent these to Mr Collier & his reply was " they cannot be

of much authority & many of them are unquestionably wrong".

:— "If all the world's a stage, and all the men & women merely players" where the devil do the audience & orchestra come from, Mr Shakespeare?! Eh! Bah! rubbish!! rot!!!" —

Surely cold neglect is better than coldst neglect – degenerate
body than derogate – Is not tie as good as elf ? – "He is
mad that trusts in the tameness of a wolf, a horses health."
Is he not madder that trusts in a horses' heels? & yet
health continues to be printed ; as well as "ten masts
at each make not the altitude which thou hast perpendicularly fell –" ten mast at least appears more
intelligible –&– May difference of opinion &—
"The first and Second Editions of Waltoni "Compleat
Angler" may be called Republican editions (1653. 55)
as on page 4 we read "All men that keep Otter dogs
should have a pension from 'the Commonwealth' altered
in the third & subsequent editions to "should have a
pension from 'the King'. –– & Shakespeares Plays. 4th ed.
1685 – "For H. Herringman, E. Brewster, R. Chiswell & R. Bentley &c"
undescribed imprint :–"For H. Herringman &c are to be sold by
Joseph Knight & Francis Saunders in the Lower walk of the New Exchange.

The Carrier's Horse:
a Coquet-side fragment.

Smales was a Carrier – what, & where he carried matters little – but Smales, being a Carrier, had a cart, and, necessarily a horse. In these Telegraphic & Railway pervading days, if Smales was not, he ought to have been – at all events his horse, being sore stricken in years, was – hors d'emploi: therefore, it was not thought expedient that he should longer cumber the earth, and consume its products. But "the veteran lagg'd superfluous on the stage", &, as he would n't voluntarily be gathered to his fathers, it was determined that he should be thither dispatched – as the cookery-books have it – "another way.". ⁓

Near to Smales's domicile, in the pleasant and picturesque village of Norsebury, lived Wattie....; the most notable fisher in the district, moreover, a keen & capital hand with the gun: he united the professions of village barber, amateur game-keeper, rod & tackle maker & purveyor of flies for such of His Majesty's lieges as were ambitious of wiling the finny denizens from the pleasant & prolific waters which skirted the village. - Next to the Carrier's very roof-tree lived old Bella Kreel, with her nephew Jimmy - a lish, keen-eyed lad of some sixteen summers - strongly imbued with the Gipsey element - nervous in speech to a degree amounting to impediment when excited, & as fond of kindred sports as Wat himself. - One fine morning the latter sallied out, gun in hand, in quest of small birds to furnish feathers for fly-dressing, Smales having previously requested him to give the old horse his quietus in the shape of a friendly bullet, & just as they had parted, Jimmy appeared on the scene, when the following conversation ensued: — "Wh-wh-wh-whaur ye gaun-W-W-Wattie, lad?" — "Oo, just to shut a few smä birds for flees." — "Wi-wi-wi-will ye let's gang w-w-wi' ye, lad?" — "Oo aye." — "H-h-h-hould on, then, till aw g-g-get my gun." All passed pleasantly for some time, & after Wat had bagged the required quantity of game, the pair approached the field where old Dobbin was standing, utterly unconscious of his impending doom, Wat having already, unknown to Jimmy, provided himself with the pre-arranged

bullet. — Under the plea of game having been
scared & scarce for the last half-hour or so, quoth
Wat, in a nonchalant manner — "Man — aw
waddent care a hä penny to shut thet horse".
"Sh-sh-sh-shut the horse, Wattie! Sh-sh-sh-
shut shut the horse! lad! — m-m-maw sang,
b-b-but but w-w-we we we'd a' be trans-
ported — we we we'd hae to f-f-f-flee the
country, lad — f-f-f-flee the country!' "
"Hoot man", cried Wat, "naebody'll ken — here's
at 'im;' & sure enough poor Dobbin succumbed
to the fatal bullet. — The effect on Jimmy
was immediate & indescribable. Consternation seized him — throwing down his gun, as
lightning he cleared a five-quarter wall —
fled like the hot-trod, scouring hedges, walls &

ditches as one possessed — leaving the herd of
swine nowhere — & never rested till breath-
lessly bursting open the door he rushed past
Bella & covered himself with the bed clothes.
Procrustes' bed to him'd been bed of down —
the Trojan horse, or Phäeton's nags as flea-
bites — 't was a calamity — a disaster — and
nothing short of transportation, or the extreme
penalty of the law presented themselves to
Jimmy's perturbed imagination. — Wattie
wending carelessly home joined the party, &
informed the Carrier (sotto voce) his mission had
been fulfilled, representing at the same time
Jimmy's dire consternation. — "God bliss us"
quoth Bella "what's oor Jimmy been deein'?
He's dune something no canny!" — "Eh, Bella"

rejoined Smales—"aw no' ken — but somebody's gaen an' shutten maw horse!" — "God bliss the lad! Shutten Smales's horse! Wor Jimmy shut a horse!"— The Carrier, stick in hand, gave three tremendous raps at Bella's door, asking, in an audible voice—"Is Jimmy in?" A smothered & agonized whine from beneath the bed-clothes feebly ejaculated "n-n-n-no, aw's n-n-not in: p-p-p-please sor, it it w-w-was n't me did it," thinking that Myrmidon of the law, the village constable, was already on his track. — It has been recorded on high authority that an hundred grey rabbits cannot make one black horse—& Smales's was a black 'un. This saw Jimmy painfully realized: indeed if such condition could

have averted the dilemma, it is certain he would have
found little difficulty in procuring the rabbits.
After some time, explanations followed: the mystery
was cleared up & a heavy load removed from the Sufferer's
breast, but even now he looks askance and feels
uneasy when any reference is made to
"The Carrier's Horse".

92

Coquet-Side

Tune:
"The Howes o' Glenorchie."

The Sun's gowden orb now dispels morning mists,
An' gaily the laverock lilts i' the sky:
The crood o' the cushats the chorus assists
Whilst the bees frae the brume to wild heatherbells fly:
The throssel noo whussels frae bonnie birk tree,
An' dew-beads are drappin frae ilka green bush,
The vilets an' gowans that sprent every brae
Wi' perfumes the sweet Simmer morn's air suffuse.

The wee lammies sport by the side o' the yowes
An' owre the lush meadows the croonin' kye stray,
Bright Phœbus wi' gowd paints the braes, fells, an' knowes,
An' sweet blushing briar buds welcome the day:
The wastlin' wind soughs thro' the saft waving corn,
An' draps frae the hedges the wat blobs o' dew,

Where e'er turns the Angler, sweet flow'rets adorn
His path — ilka step rural pleasures accrue.

———

The clear, wimplin' burnie rows on its fair course
'Enchanting his soul wi' it sweet melodie:
On ilka side Nature wi' him haulds discourse,
An' frae a' warldly cares feels his conscience is free:
The foxgloves an' gowden whuns bow to the breeze
 An' wild roses wantonly try to ensnare
Wi' their sweet scented May-buds th' wanderin' bees,
An' hawthorn's snaw-blossoms perfume the sweet air.

———

The twittering ouzel frae stane to stane flits,
Wi' his dusky gray jacket an snawy white throat:
The hern-seugh his eyrie for scaly fry quits,
 An' ilk feather'd chorister tunes up his note.
What joys then around us on ilka side seen,
 An' wha wadna' follow this charmin' pursuit

He that cares na' to worship auld Nature's fair Queen,
May aye be weel pleas'd wi' a creelfu' o' troot.

Jos Crawhall Jun: Delt 1880.

Baldus & Zankar: a Legend of Holystone.

"HOLYSTONE, a desolate little hamlet among the hills, seven miles west of Rothbury. A path leads across a meadow from the village to a little grove of firs enclosing "Our Lady's Well," a square basin of transparent emerald-green water, with a copious spring. An old moss grown statue of an Ecclesiastic stands on the brink, and rising from the water is a tall cross, with the inscription:— "In this place Paulinus the Bishop baptized 3000 Northumbrians, Easter, DCXXVII."— It is an interesting & striking spot, & well worthy of a visit. The little Church stands on the site of a small convent for 8 Benedictine nuns. The remains of a stone cross still exist upon the moors between this & Elsdon, which was a station of prayer for pilgrims coming to Holystone." Handbook North? 1864

"God speed the good Paulinus in his holy work of love,
God speed him & his convert flock_ all blessings from above

'Esther – a Cantata.. Voice from audience :– "Hi! I say. don't cut it too fat".
Ahasuerus, (coming to the front):– "Now you look 'ere – this ere's a
Solemn piece – an' I'm Ahasuerus – but ven the Cantata's over
I'm Jim Smith – an if that Gennelman as don't want it cut too fat'll
come round 'ere arter the piece, I'll cut it fat for 'im – I will." –

Light on this earnest, godly man, & on each neophyte
Now thoroughly regenerate – illumed by the true light".
Thus pray'd two saintly Fathers who to Holystone had come.
One Baldus hight, Zankar his frere "par nobile fratrum":
Their mission heathen to convert, & heathens' souls to save,
By conjuring heathen bodies in the Holy well to lave.
With fasts & vigils shriven. Saint Baldus was a hollow man,

Pious and godly, wise and grave, in sooth a very solemnium.
Zankar the like, tho' truth to tell, a bronzed and ruddy
                                                          hue.

And 'en bon point' belied the fasts he'd vow'd to have kept true:
No matter. Rumours blatant trumps blows strange reports about,
Bankar was still a godly man - he had'nt been found out.
Full many a weary mile they'd trudged, & prodigal of heat
Old Sol his rays sent fiercely down - the Fathers rest to eat:
Their frugal meal of simplest fare demands but scanty words,
The fragments gather'd with great care to feed the dicky birds.
In holy conversation then - & meditation deep
Some time they pass, till Baldus, worn & weary, drops asleep:
Bankar as well nods thoughtfully & slowly droops his eyes,
And in their turn they each become a banquet for the flies.
The elder Saint sleeps placidly - for Bankar there's no rest,
Whether his conscience or the flies, the holy man knew best:
Still Baldus slept, most soundly slept - not so his wakeful frere,
And a most unholy, hideous stench pervades the atmosphere.
'Tis true no longer Baldus felt annoyance from the flies,
But a feeling much more horrible assail'd his nose and eyes:

A pungent exhalation rose, apparent, from the ground,
And o'er his haggard cheeks the briny tears trickled down.
In horror woke the saintly man & agoniz'd cried out,
"Now sure the foul fiend walks the earth." Zankar was near
found out!

But craftily & cunningly he hides the peccant clay,
Ejaculating inward – "What'll Missus Grundy say?".
"Now, by the rood" quoth Baldus, pale. "I'm sick unto the death,
The foul fiend's stench pervades my limbs & takes away my breath."

'Tis well I quaff'd the crystal Spring, & ate unto Satiety

(For Beelzebub a flavour now confers on our society."

Bankar, his conscience smiting him, then cried with trembling voice

"Don't look at me - thou holy man, in such a tone of voice."

Confused he was, full sore abash'd - unable long to speak -

"Concealment, like a worm i' the bud prey'd on his damask cheek."

"Confess'd I stand before thee now, a culprit" - thus he spoke -

"To screen thy placid countenance from flies I rais'd a smoke.

"'Twas thus" - & from his scrip he drew a tube of virgin clay

(Fill'd to the brim with noisome weed, the flies to drive away.

"To it a spark of holy fire, unwitting, I applied,

With suction kept the weed alight - the pests by thousands died:

now nay! now nay! thou holy man - I did it for thy good,

And not one single insect's left to drain thy dear heart's blood".

After much subtle argument & practick explanation,

The holy saint felt half convinced & - tried an inhalation:

Then Zankar, to complete the test, secured an errant fly,
And plainly proved "when Doctors differ patients surely die."
"Now for thy great discovery, good Zankar, rest forgiven,
For future ages' benefit thou of thy sins art shriven".
A noisome weed indeed it was, (but, singular to say,
That many holy Fathers since at flies have blazed away.')

With fervent mind & pious thought (their bodies rested well)
Proceeded now the Fathers to Our Lady's Holy well,
That em'rald well by fragrant firs protected on each side,
Within a lovely pleasaunce by Paulinus Sanctified:
The heathen pilgrims come in streams adown the heath-clad hill
And joyously the twain commence their mission to fulfil,
From early morn to dusky eve, nigh knee-deep in the wave,
The sacred rites administer, Northumbers' souls to save:
The ceremony ended, after Vespers, all disperse,
And the Fathers, not improperly, on world's affairs converse.
The kindly fire now sparkles, & the frugal board is spread,
Roots, eleemosyn milk & corn, with herbs & driest bread,
No honied mead, no humming ale the pious Fathers bring,
But temperately quench their thirst at Saint Paulinus' spring:
And so to rest - hail! balmy sleep - but Baldus, rack't with pain,
Lay restless on his leafy couch - to slumber tried in vain -

When, lo! a cough & sneeze betray'd the fiend on earth once more,
Quoth Baldus, "whence proceeds that stench at this untimely hour?
You know, good Bankar, in the night no flies do buzz about,
The cool & chilly evening air puts all their tribes to rout:
Pray tell the cause that I may sleep – I'm pained & ill at ease".
"For information" quoth the frere, "I'm trying 't on the fleas!"
Then Baldus was a wrathful man, & madly tore his hair,
That is, he would have torn it, but, alas! – he'd none to tear.
Upspringing from his rustic bed, & madly twing'd with pain
A horrid war-dance danced – turn'd ill – & then lay down again.
A baleful fever had set in – no skilful leech was nigh,
Bankar, with sorrowing look regards the Father's glazing eye:
(No simples now avail his case, no roots or herbs of use,)
He prompt puts back existence' clock to the time when he was loose:
Diving again into his scrip, which stands him in good stead,
A curious vessel he drew forth, most cunning shaped in lead,

"Then Baldus
was a wrathful man.

The top was fastened with a screw, & at the foot a cup,
The latter with it's contents fill'd — Saint Baldus drank it up,
Then mark the change, the wholesome change, upon the dying man,
His eyes 'gan twinkle, & his tongue most eloquently ran —
"By thrones & dominations — by all the powers above —
By Jove & all the heathen gods — by a good Christian's love,
Repeat the dose, skill'd Zankar — Oh! fill the cup again,
That potent potion's soothing taste alleviates my pain —
Has Galen — or Hippocrates left the foul Stygian shore?
Oh! Shade of Æsculapius — fill — fill the cup once more.
It courses through my languid blood, I feel't in every vein,"
And, maudlin, he held out his hand — "Oh! fill the cup again!
Fill, fill the cup — I'll drink it up, e'en though it be my death."
The Father took another pull, & gasp'd for want of breath:
A rambling, ghastly pun he made, in spirit sore subdued,
"Bhankar! the vesshel ish a screw — I've drank it an' I'm sorewed!"

A while he slept, woke quite refresh'd — Spent some time in devotion,
But no man to this day has learnt the compound of that potion.
[Here the Manuscript has, unfortunately, suffered
. . . from damp, & is illegible . . . . .]

No holy vigils kept that night — they burnt no midnight oil,
But Zankar & Saint Baldus slumbered — à la belle étoile.

The Awakening & the Doom

With half-averted, blear-eyed look, the Fathers sad awoke,
Repentant of their revelry but neither a word spoke,
When Saint Paulinus suddenly appear'd in wrathful mood
And thus address'd the peccant, yet half conscious brotherhood: —

"I will not aggravate your sins by recapitulation
But much too light a punishment is excommunication,
Hear then your doom – first Bankar list! as the most erring man,
That wanly the unsuspecting Baldus did trepan –
Thy vigils as a Statue Keep on brink of Holy well
Till penitent thou hearst the sound of Convent's passing bell:
Baldus for aye a troubled shade shall roam the country wide
And a record Keep of all events that hap on Coquet-side."
Certes, no rest that shadow gets, pass'd daily thro' the post,
And still a moss-grown Statue marks the place of Bankar's
GHOST. ~

Coquet-Side:
the Wife's remonstrance.

Tune.—
'Todlin hame'.

Chorus

Ye brought me to Coquet to giė me a treat,
An' I canna but say, we've had plenty to eat:
But as for the whusky-ye ken whaes had that
An' yer fishin's a' meunshine I'll just tell ye flat.

Chorus.— Potterin' on - potterin' on -
Ye've no catch't a troot a' day-potterin' on.

When we started this mornin' ye said ye wad sit -
But it's aye the auld gam'-the poor wife maun submit-

Ye've been floggin' a' day - barely time for a meal -
An' a' ye've to show for't's that rubbishin' eel.
  Potterin' on - potterin' on -
   Brag nae mair o' big troots wi' yer potterin' on.

Ye've oft tell't me Coquet-side's bonnie an' bright,
An' ye'd fish yer frien's round, owther number or weight,
What ye'd catch if the wind but keptoot o' the East -
Hoots! let's hyem - for "eneugh's just as good as a feast."
  Potterin' on - potterin' on -
   Sang! it will be a feast wi' yer potterin' on.

The bairns'll be starvin' - the fire clean oot,
An' we'll niver get hyem if we wait for that troot -
Sae put up yer gad an' unfettle yer reel,
An' be thankful ye've gotten that kizzen'd ahd eel.
  Potterin' on - potterin' on,

I'm as seik as a pyett wi' yer potterin' on.

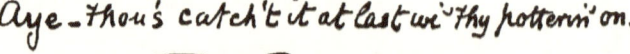

"Eh! hinny – ane cast just ayont that big stane,
For to get the bit bairnies a supper I'm fain –
A grand troot's just risen – they're strang on the feed,"
I'll hev him next thraw – but – he plopt ower heed."
Potterin' on – potterin' on –
Aye – thou's catch't it at last wi' thy potterin' on.

July 12. 1880.

The Angler's toast.

Tune: "The general toast."

Drink, my boys, drink to the Sports o' the field
 Drink to the Pad, Gun, an' Stable :
 Each to its devotee pleasure does yield,
 Not the least the glad 'meet' round the table .
  Let each drink his glass
  To his favourite lass,
 I hope eighty lang years they thegither may pass.

How joyous to Hunters the sound o' the horn :
 To the Lads o' the trigger the whirrin'
 O' pheasant frae thicket or paitrick frae corn :
 To the Fisher his braw brass wheel birrin'.
  Chorus again,
  We agree i' the main,
 Sae rattle the rafters till a' ring again.

Ilk brither's accorded his favour'd pursuit;
　Success to his honest endeavour,
Be't hunting, or shooting, or heuking a trout,
　The sports of auld England for ever!
　　For Nimrod, hurrah!
　　Ramrod an' a'—
Langrod an' red heckle can fettle them a'.

———

Tally ho! then, Old Towler, see how Reynard flies,
　To ho! Ponto—down charge—be steady!
'I have him' quoth Langrod—an' troutie sure dies,
　Our watch word in every sport's—ready.
　　Your glasses then fill,
　　An' bumpers we'll smill:
Let each follow his bent wi'a hearty good will.

———

Coquet-side's been the scene of our aft joyous meet:
  Time ne'er can it's memories sever;
  Frae Warkworth to Barraburn's lanely retreat,
  The Coquet for aye an' for ever!
      Weldon's auld Ha'!
      Felton an' a'—
  Rothbury, Hepple, an' bonnie Wood ha'.

May our hearts be o' happiness full as our creels,
  As our journey thro' life it will sweeten,
  Ane toast 'fore we part- fill a bumper- nae heels
  And - here's to "our next merrie meetin'!"
      Chorus again —
      We agree i' the main —
  An'— now it is time we were "toddlin' hame."

The Choice of Paris: ~~an Idle~~
an Idyl. —

Paris was the second son of Priam & Hecuba. Before his birth Hecuba dreamt that she had brought forth a fire-brand, the flames of which spread over the whole city. Accordingly, as soon as the child was born, he was given to a shepherd, who was to expose him on Mount Ida. After the lapse of 5 days, the shepherd, on returning to Mount Ida, found the child still alive, & fed by a she-bear: thereupon he carried the boy home & brought him up with his own child, & called him Paris. When Paris had grown up, he distinguished himself as a valiant defender of the flocks & shepherds.... Once upon a time, when Peleus & Thetis solemnized their nuptials, all the gods were invited to the marriage, with the exception of Eris, or Strife. Enraged at her exclusion, the goddess threw a golden apple among the guests, with the inscription "TO THE FAIREST". — Thereupon Juno, Venus & Minerva each claimed the apple for herself. Jupiter ordered Mercury to take the goddesses to Mount Gargarus, a portion of Ida, to the beautiful shepherd Paris, who was there tending his

flocks, & who was to decide the dispute. Juno promised him the
sovereignty of Asia & great riches, Minerva great glory & renown in
war, & Venus the fairest of women for his wife. Paris decided in
favour of Venus. (Dynamite). Paris sailed to Greece under the
protection of Venus". — Smith's Classical Dictionary. —

Prologue. —

When these events occurred, King Priam's son,
The valiant Hector, 'd reached the age of – one!
A lone young Trojan. – Hecuba, his mother,
Invoked Lucina for a little brother:
Such invocations seldom are in vain,
And in due time the little beggar came.
(Mind, brats in verse are difficult to bear,
But, now we've got him – let's trace his career:)
That he would be a fire-brand & a Tartar
His mother'd dreamt – then fain he'd been a daughter,
For, in her clairvoyance, she saw the boy

A conflagration raise that burnt all Troy.
To Priam Hecuba had told her dream,
And they, conjointly, hatch a wicked scheme
To rid the world of this incendious mite,
And - will I, nill I - put him out of sight.
Well may be asked - "What's Hecuba to him,
Or he to Hecuba?" - poor little limb!
Well might young hopeful stare - so early done for
And wonder what on earth he'd been begun for.
Stern Priam exercised his royal sway,
And the doomed child was ruthless torn away
To meet his fate - when Hecuba, o'ercome
Suggested present banishment from home
To some lone place where him they'd ne'er set eyes on;
A kindlier fate than drowning, sword or poison.
"Come, Hecuba, my Queen - your feelings stifle,
(Seldom in those days kings stuck at a trifle:)

Since putting down the brat gives so much pain,
We'll put him out to some kind shepherd swain,
Some rustic Damon who'll no doubt receive him,
With hints substantial that we mean to leave him.
Such rustic - Dæmon call him - soon appearēd,
And with the youngster quickly disappeared -
Away from Troy straight with his charge he hied,
Secured a doubtful "Patmos" on Mount Ide -
There left to cruel fate - nay, chill undoing,
But for a nice mild bear - a nappy bruin,

Most fitting beast to bear the name of Beauty,
For kindly she discharged a mother's duty,
Washed, fed & dressed – ah! but where's the robing?
Leaves from some old edition of "Cock Robin!"

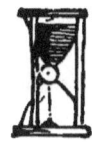

(Day glasses.)

The Shepherd, Sheepish, went his weekly round –
And, lo! the brat alive & kicking found:
With dire amazement was well nigh struck dumb:
The boy goo-googled, grinned, & sucked his thumb:
Clod's cruel heart relents – he takes him home,
And from this time adopts him as his own –
Gave him the name of Paris, so that none
Could ever know he'd farmed King Priam's son.
. . . . (probably a Greek Kalend.) . . . .

Deck't with straw hat, gay ribbons, crook, pipe from old Pan,
(He'd the peacock stage reached of each dressy young man,
A stage we all pass through in life's short career,
When we're not apt to think ourselves "very small beer".
Thus he tended his flocks – Studied hard in Bucolics,
Led a pastoral life quite away from Town's frolics –

(Such existence immaculate only __rus__ yields
In cowslippery, lush, buttercuppery fields:)
Tootled on his oat-pipe with such exquisite strain
That we'll let him toot on till we want him again.

• • • • • • • • • • •

Play.

High jinks on Olympus - a grand gala day -
All the gods there assembled in brilliant array :
The primary cause of this great nuptial meetis,
The wedding of Peleus with lovely Miss Thetis.
Such flaunting of ribbons - saltatory paces,
White grenades, orange blossoms, & Honiton laces,
Such flirting, & blushing, & treading on skirts,
By gods wearing sandals & very short shirts:
So much jigging & junketing - nectar - ambrosia -
That the happy pair (tired) gan to wish themselves cozier:
Apollo twang'd string'ly his tortoise shell lyre,
While Pan on his syrinx blew higher & higher,
The Muses as well formed a sweet choral crew
And in soft diapasons mild Zephyrus blew:
The blushing brides trousers - beg pardon - trousseau
Caused with jealousy scanty dress'd damselst'o'erflow
And a feeble attempt's made herein to compress

A list of the presents prepared for "the press": —
"Christian years," & Church Services, blankets & fans,
Lace flounces, mouchoir cases, brass warming pans
Sachets & salt cellars, rings, lockets in swarms,
And a feather quilt cosey to keep the pair warm:
Corals with silver bells, salvers, ormolu clocks,
£30. and a bundle of wee babbie's smocks,
Fine rococo ornaments — Knit muffatees,
Glove stretchers — gridirons — an ominous cheese —
A gilt aneroid & some splendid lace shifts,
With a great many more, were, as usual, gifts.

. . . .

A host of old shoes was all ready to throw
When the festive proceedings received a sad blow
By the sudden descent of a turbulent wife,
Who sent in her card — "Madame Evis, née Strife,"
And demanded immediate & clear explanation

Why she'd been excluded - had no invitation -
"Vile upstarts - I'll teach you my presence to slight -
I'm of very old family - Daughter of Night -
Naught akin to your Jenkinses & nouveaux riches,
Who'd fain try "Society" manners to teach -
If I join not your revels then woe you betide."
The gods stood dumfounded, but no one replied -
She this tacit hint took but before she   withdrew,
An apple of gold in the midst of   them threw -
The "Apple of Discord" - of fruits   happ'ly rarest,
On the rind in bold letters inscribed "TO   THE FAIREST."
To the front quick a bevy of goddesses   rushed,
Soon their back hair all down & their crinolines crushed,
On Olympus such scrambles had never been seen,
'Twixt Venus, Minerva, & Heaven's great Queen,
When Jupiter thundered in terrible huff -
"Pray give me that apple - enough, girls, enough -

"D'ye think it's respectable this crowdie-main?
Juno – Venus – Minerva – I pray you refrain,
Give at once up the apple – let me have it from ye
A racket like this is fair Hades an' Tommy!
You'll bring great discredit upon my domain,
Give it up at once, Juno – you old harridan:
It's really too bad that all miseries human
Should arise from a mixture of apples & woman,
For it is n't so long since, you very well know,
Through this very same fruit Adam had such a row –
To be sure in his case there was no competition,
Whilst in ours there's no chance of an equal partition,
So I'll send you with Mercury all to Gargarus
To be bound by the final decision of Paris".
The ladies were pacified – each one agreed
That before the young shepherd her own cause would plead.

. . . .

ON a pleasant green slope, overshadowed by trees,
The three anxious goddesses wait their decrees :
The Shepherd sat stolid - majestically frowned,
And - as high priest oracular looked quite profound.

Great Juno then, first by prerogative spoke,
And in sweet, silvered accents did Paris invoke -
"Tho' I'm fat, fair & forty - great Jupiters wife
'Tis admitted I ne'er looked so well in my life,
And I think, gentle Shepherd, you'll also agree
That the eyes of all nations are centred on me.
I have fabulous riches - broad acres of land
All in my own right at my ready command:
I can make or unmake - create Kaiser or King
And to those who show kindness I steadily cling -
Think this no intimation that I'll befriend you
Tho' I now have on hand a spare Kingdom or two,

With armies & armaments – rich mines galore,
Coin, jewell'ry, plate, & know not what more:
Just a hint – that Town Councillors I make at will,
And, by stretching a point, can the Civic chair fill.
Then think, gentle Paris, before you decree
What might hap if the apple should roll towards me."

. . . .

. . . .

Still stolid & Sphinx-like did Paris appear,
And tacitly hinted Athena he'd hear.

. . . .

Half-smiling, half-stern, to bewilder the Swain,
Minerva commenced her harangue in this strain –
"No bribe avails me as with truculent men,
Bet baksheesh – Tip – trink-gelt – pour-boire – pot de vin,
Leave we such for M.P.'s, & for those who seek places,
Hope for glory in war, great renown – mental graces:

Yet no harm can arise from a quiet display
Of a few little things I might throw in thy way:
Thus - a £30. charger thou stately might straddle
With "plated goods" dangling each side o' the saddle -
Might sleep in thy uniform - always wear spurs,
(To salvation in plain clothes the soldier demurs),
Have a shiny steel scabbard, & real drawn sword,
Nay - e'en serve in serve in same corps with a real live LORD
Exceeding in all respects each "tinsel Don"
Of our phalanx of Marses - nineteen to the ton:
And should e'er thy great mind seek relief from the wars

In an undress might lounge, smoke toothpicks & cigars,
Then last, tho' not least - be't with bated breath said -
Thou might start a small flunkey with "Such a cockade",

And in all respects
look like a true Son
of Mars,
With the option of
leaving in case of
real wars.
If as eager with
these as with foes
thou would'st grapple,
I pr'y thee, sweet
Paris - award me the apple."

The pleased Shepherd smiled with ineffable grace,
But none yet a clue to his judgment could trace.

The Goddess of Love next came tripping along
Like Breitmann's famed maiden "vot's got nodings on":
Then, how Juno did frown - chaste Minerva looked glum,
While Paris he twiddled his finger and thumb,
Abstracted gazed Sky ward - then on the horizon,
Unobserved, peeped askance where he'd fain rest his eyes on,
Conscience stricken with qualms that he'd ever presided,
As he felt that the case was already decided.
"Aroint - shameless hussy" quoth Juno, enraged -
"Is this a fair war, so immodestly waged?
Away from our presence - thy time quick dow -
The court is adjourned & awaits thee anon".
Appalled by the goddess, then Venus retired,
Eftsoons reappearing - yet slightly attired:
For addition above there was still ample room,
And her garment below left off terribly soon .
Then the charming young shepherd she wantonly eyed,

And thus spoke — in theatrical parlance — 'aside' —
"Why should old frumps like these to my dress take exception,
I'm bound they're both made up, a mass of deception:
Moreover, how can you judge any one's points
With their pepli & tunics enshrouding their joints?
Let's have every thing real — do nothing by halves,
You might make a pin-cushion of Juno's fat calves:
And as for Minerva's great helmet — 'tis said
She just wears it to cover a very bald head:
They're all padding — false bosoms — false hips — & false — well,
What else they have false I'd much rather not tell:
(Fictions founded on fact or my senses belie,
Now I'm all over fact — just you nip me and try."
(THIS SETTLED THE SHEPHERD.) — Then Venus aloud,
With a triumphant air looking round on the crowd —
"No bribe do I offer — give Nature her bent,
Then choose thee a wife to thy heart's own content,

Thy life, Spring eternal last all the year round,
And no thorn in thy path save from love's pleasant wound:
Thine no lot as on earth where youth, beauty, are sold
To some old shoddy Crœsus all stinking of gold,
Her heart a mere purse – She a blind Devotee
To that great triune idol – that God £. s. d.
No – I swear by my chastity – by the Lord Harry –
Thou of women the fairest created shalt marry,
And with every good gift shall thy bride be endowed,
So – rely on me, Paris 🍎 I've already vowed."

The Shepherd still smiled when he heard her begin:
While she spoke it relaxed to a visible grin –
Her oration complete – yet another sweet smile:
Joint permission received to consider a while:
Then a very short season the Session adjourned,
Whilst his final Decision each eagerly yearned.
· · · · · · · · · · · ·

The Court reassembled - with simpering gaze
All three to the Shepherd expectant eyes raise -
The Queen'd fain address him, a feeler to try,
But the others soon crippled her "ballon d'essai":
"Do not touch Fortune's rudder - no secrets reveal,
'Tis forbidden to speak to the 'man at the wheel'."
A decorous silence the guests then displayed,
Quoth Paris - "Your merits I've carefully weighed -
But I do feel so nervous - great Jove come between us -
My life's in your hands - and - the apple's for Venus."

Like evil yeast working in contracted brain,
Then Minerva & Juno ferment with disdain -
Jocund Strife hovered nigh with a pestilent yell,
Which triple-tongued Cerberus echoed from hell.
Paralyzed was the earth, & incontinent hills

Quaked with fear & ran down in impetuous rills,
Which, as rivers rushed on sweeping all in their courses
Till terrified, turned & ran back to their sources.
The heavens were darkened — the world stood still —
Trees withered — rocks burrowed o'er head in each hill —
Yells of fury arose in a horrible clamour
And o'er the earth's surface shed chaotic glamour.

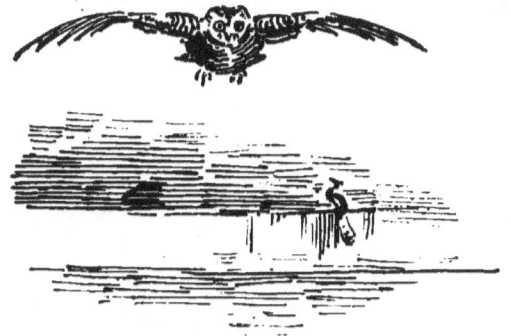

The wise bird of Pallas shriek'd one death hoo! hoo!
And away to the caves of Mount Gargarus flew,
While Juno's gay peacock collapsed his starr'd tail,

156

And the mountain air rent with a hideous wail.

. . . .

Unsafe on Mount Ida, & yearning for peace,
The Goddess of Love embarked forthwith for Greece,
Soft & prosperous gales gaily wafted her thither
And the Histories say that she took Paris with her.
For the rest of the deeds of this 'broth of a boy',
See your Lexicons — articles "PARIS" and "TROY".

The Hunt ys upp.

Sayth Salamons songe / fayre aege and longe /
Is mayde by a Spyryte goode /
And syth it is soo / to your dysportes goo /
By streme or merrie grene wood.
The Huntyrs horne wakes upp the morne /
and hawk bells sounde on hye /
The Foulere hath sped from his sorrye bed:
Dooth the laggard Fysshere lye?

To myn entent / the Hontyre hys bente /
  Entayleth too moche labore :
Wete shode and myred / cloathes torne / & tyred /
  Lyppes blysterred / swetynge sore .
Then Hawkynge too / noyouse alsoo /
  And ofte ryghte euyll a thurste :
Gette Rye or Cray / or flye awaye /
  Thoghe he whystel tyll he burste .
Ynn Wynter colde the Foulere bolde
  Settyth his gynne and snare /
The morne-tyde dewe dooth wete hym throo /
  Ande soryly dooth he fayre .
Moore cowde be sayd / but holsome drede
  Of magre makith me leve :
Nedes be the beste sorte of alle dysporte
  Ys fysshe wyth an hoke to deceive .

139

For alle mooste maye be broke/a lyne or an hoke/
Home mayde hee hathe plentee more/
Soe the Fysshere hys losse ys notte greuous
Gyf of troughtes hee hathe good store.
——◉——
And mery at ease on eche ryde he sees
Melodyous fowles of the ayre/
Whyle spontaneous he/affectuously
Sayth his custumable prayer.
——◉——

1480

Chorus:—
Synge - (The Hunt ys uppe/ the Hunt ys upp/
(For Coney or byrde on the tree/
Alle the foure dysportes are goode of theyr Sortes/
Butte - Angle fysshynge for me.
—— ☉ ——

1880.

(50 Copies) - Imprinted by Andrew Reid for the author,
& are to be sold by Robert Robinson - Bewick's head -
Pilgrim Street - Newcastle upon Tyne. Price 3 guineas.

plates destroyed
Andrew Reid

Author:- "I say - Reader - Can you tell me if that young
man comes on again?"
Reader:- "Of course he does - frequently - Why that's Hamlet."
Author:- "Oh! then I'm off - Good bye." -

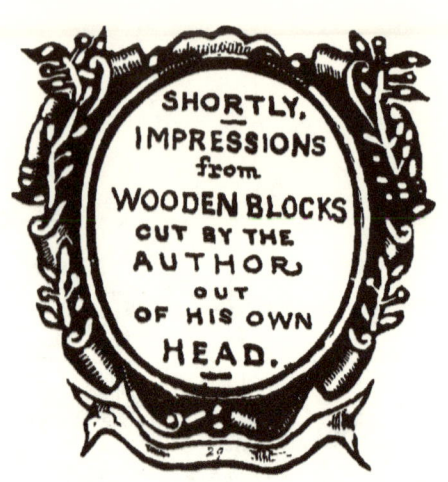

SHORTLY,
—
IMPRESSIONS
from
WOODEN BLOCKS
CUT BY THE
AUTHOR
OUT
OF HIS OWN
HEAD.